GREAT ILLUSTRATED CLASSICS

DR. JEKYLL AND MR. HYDE

Robert Louis Stevenson

adapted by
Mitsu Yamamoto

Illustrations by
Pablo Marcos Studio

BARONET
BOOKS

BARONET BOOKS, New York, New York

GREAT ILLUSTRATED CLASSICS

edited by
Malvina G. Vogel

Contents

Robert Louis Stevenson

About the Author

Robert Louis Stevenson was born in Edinburgh, Scotland, in 1850. He was a frail child, who was greatly influenced by his father's punishments and by his nurse's horrifying tales of demons.

Stevenson refused to follow the family profession of engineering and chose law when he went to the University of Edinburgh to study. But he soon gave that up and turned to writing, which his poor health could not deter.

After he married an American woman, Stevenson and his devoted wife traveled throughout the world trying to improve his delicate health while he continued his writing. In the four years between 1883 and 1887, Stevenson wrote his four longest and greatest novels: *Treasure Island, The Black Arrow, The Strange Case of Dr. Jekyll and Mr. Hyde,* and *Kidnapped,* and his famous book of poems, A *Child's Garden of Verses.*

The Strange Case of Dr. Jekyll and Mr. Hyde was born in a nightmare, but Stevenson remembered enough of it when he awoke to get it down on paper. Within three days he had the entire first draft written. He intended this book not only as a "thriller," but also as a study of good and evil, which are always at war within man.

Stevenson and his family spent his last years on the South Pacific island of Samoa, where he continued his writing until he collapsed and died in 1894... at the young age of forty-four.

People You Will Read About

Dr. Henry Jekyll, *a medical doctor and scientist*

Edward Hyde, *Jekyll's mysterious friend and heir*

Gabriel John Utterson, *Jekyll's old friend and lawyer*

Hastie Lanyon, *Jekyll's childhood friend and doctor*

Poole, *Jekyll's butler*

Richard Enfield, *Mr. Utterson's young cousin*

Inspector Newcomen, *a Scotland Yard detective*

Mr. Guest, *head law clerk to Mr. Utterson*

Sir Danvers Carew, *a Member of Parliament*

Sarah, a *housemaid*

An Offer of a Cab

CHAPTER 1

A Child in the Night

Two well-dressed men were about to cross a London street on a sunny Sunday morning. They were Mr. Gabriel John Utterson, an elderly lawyer, and his young cousin, Richard Enfield. A horse-drawn hansom cab drew up beside them, and the cabman leaned down from his perch, waving his whip.

"Mornin', gentlemen," the cabman called with a hopeful smile. "Off to church on this fine Sunday, I'll bet. I'll have you there in two winks or less."

Mr. Utterson never spoke unless it was

important. He frowned at the cabman and waved him away. But Richard gave the man a friendly smile and shook his head.

"No, my good man, we are out for a walk, which we take every Sunday. That's the way to see interesting things in London."

They crossed several streets and soon found themselves in a dingy neighborhood. As they slowly walked down a small street full of shops, Mr. Utterson stopped to admire an interesting display in a store window.

Suddenly Richard tugged at his sleeve and spoke with a serious note in his voice. "See that door across the street, Cousin? It is involved with something rather odd that happened to me."

Mr. Utterson looked at the scarred, weatherbeaten door Richard was pointing to. It belonged to a two-story building that was one of several built around a courtyard. Because there were no windows at the front of the

A Scarred, Weather-Beaten Door

building, it looked deserted and somewhat sinister.

Mr. Utterson's usually indifferent tone of voice took on a note of curiosity. "Indeed? What is that door to you?" he asked.

Richard drew him back against the storefront and spoke softly. "I was coming home alone from a party on a dark winter night. There were some lights in the street, but no people. Everyone was asleep, and I heard only my own footsteps. Not far from here, as I neared an intersection, I suddenly saw two people. One, coming up one street, was a little girl, running as hard as she could. And coming up a side street was a short figure of a man, clumping along at a good rate. I saw they were bound to collide at the corner, but there was nothing I could do. It happened very fast. They met with a bang, and the child was knocked off her feet. I heard her cry out. By that time, I was running toward

Bound To Collide at the Corner

them to help in any way that I could."

Richard was so caught up in his story that he did not notice his cousin looking almost fearful as he listened. If he had noticed, he would have stopped talking, and been astonished, for Gabriel John Utterson rarely displayed his emotions, even to his many friends.

Richard spoke faster now, his eyes flashing. "The man had the wind knocked out of him for a moment. But instead of picking the child up, he—you will find this hard to believe, Cousin, but I swear it is true—he trampled on her! Stamped right on her and over her, and continued on his way! The child's screams were terrible. I raced after the man and seized him by his coat collar. The face he turned to me was one hideous snarl, and for a crazed moment, I wondered if this was a man or an animal!"

"He Trampled on Her!"

Only Bruised, but Badly Frightened

CHAPTER 2

"Blackmail House"

"Did this... this creature struggle with you?" asked Mr. Utterson.

"No," answered Richard. "He was almost unconcerned. He offered no resistance as I led him back to the child. By this time, a group of people had gathered, summoned by her screams. They included the child's family, who lived two houses down from the corner. In a moment, we were joined by the doctor whom the child had been sent to fetch because her mother was sick. He pronounced her only bruised, but badly frightened.

THE STRANGE CASE OF
DR. JEKYLL AND MR. HYDE

"All this time I kept a tight hold on my man, though he was so repulsive, I hated to touch him. I could see the others hated him too, for his appearance as well as for what he had done. Even the doctor, who is accustomed to terrible sights, drew away from him."

"Why? Was he deformed?" asked Mr. Utterson. "Or scarred on his face?"

Richard shook his head. "No, but there was a *feeling* of deformity about him. He looked like everyone else and yet he did not. There was something strange and detestable about his appearance. I cannot be more precise than that. Perhaps his manner was evil, so that he brought hatred on himself."

"But what about the door? You said your adventure involved that door across the street," reminded the lawyer, who was used to bringing people back to the point of a story.

"Yes, I'm coming to that," said Richard. "We all made such a fuss, threatening to blacken

"I Kept a Tight Hold on My Man."

his name throughout London with a description of his actions that the man lost some of his coolness. He became a bit frightened though he tried to hide it. At last he offered money to the child's family. Only a few pounds at first. But finally we got him up to a hundred pounds in exchange for our silence. Of course, he was not carrying such a large sum on him. So he led the child's father, the doctor, and myself to that very door. He whipped out a key and went in. When he came out, he had ten pounds in gold and the rest in a check.

"But here, Cousin, is the mystery, for the check was signed by a very well-known man. I will not mention his name because he is important in his profession and is also highly respected for his good works.

"Of course, we objected that the check must be a forgery. But the creature said he could stay with us until the bank opened in the morning and then take us with him so he

Ten Pounds in Gold and a Check

could cash the check in our presence."

Mr. Utterson's face was sad as he turned away from his cousin and said, "The check was good, I am sure."

"Yes," said Richard eagerly. "I was coming to that. Well, it being early, I took everyone back to my rooms until morning, fed them breakfast, and then we went in a body to the bank. The check was cashed without the faintest objection, and the man calmly handed the money over to the child's father as if he gave away a hundred pounds every day. But since it was not his money, what did it matter to him?

"So I call that house across the street 'Blackmail House.' That door must be a cellar entrance to the home of this important citizen that I dare not name. This evil person must have some hold over the owner. In short, he must be blackmailing him."

Richard stopped talking on this triumphant

Handing the Money to the Child's Father

note, and the two men resumed their stroll. But Mr. Utterson was not finished with the topic.

"Did you try to find out why the signer of the check was being blackmailed?" he asked, pretending an indifferent tone.

"No," said Richard. "I didn't want to know any more of the matter. I happened to read in the newspaper one day the address of that important man. It is in some square or other right in this area. If that door leads to a passageway to his house at the address I read, I don't care to know for sure. The houses in that courtyard are so pushed together, it is hard to say where one begins and another ends. No, if the man has a guilty secret, which he pays to keep hidden, then I surely am not one to try and sniff it out." Richard nodded his head in self-approval.

Mr. Utterson was not done yet. "You are sure the blackmailer used a key?" he asked,

Walking and Talking

using something of his courtroom manner.

"Cousin, I have said so," answered Richard, surprised to be doubted. "In fact, I passed here last week and saw him use the key again to open that door. Oh, he has a key, make no mistake about that."

Mr. Utterson sighed deeply. "Richard, aren't you surprised that I do not press you to reveal the name on the check?"

"Yes, I am," admitted the younger man. "I would be eaten up by curiosity if I were you. I suppose that as one grows older, one wants fewer surprises. Is that it?"

Mr. Utterson shook his head. "No. I do not ask the name because I already know it."

Richard halted abruptly. "You know it?"

Mr. Utterson had continued walking and now he looked back, motioning Richard to follow. "Yes, I'm afraid I do. Your decision not to look further into the matter does you credit.

Utterson Knows the Name on the Check.

Perhaps your good intentions not to meddle in the lives of others should extend to not passing on gossip, as you have done today."

Richard flushed. "You are right, of course. I talk too much. Well, I will make a promise never to refer to this incident again. Does that suit you?"

The lawyer smiled fondly at his young cousin. "Yes, except for one thing. Before the promise goes into effect, will you answer one question about the incident?"

"To you, certainly."

With an effort of will, Mr. Utterson kept his voice from trembling as he asked, "Do you know the name of the man who entered that door with a key, the one who trampled the child?"

"Yes, of course," answered Richard. "He told us his name was Mr. Hyde."

Mr. Hyde!

Taking Dr. Jekyll's Will from the Safe

CHAPTER 3

Dr. Jekyll's Will

Usually Mr. Utterson was in good spirits after his Sunday walk with his cousin. He enjoyed the sunny nature of the younger man as well as his fresh opinions. But tonight, Utterson was somber. He ate his dinner without enjoyment, causing his cook to wonder if she had undercooked the beef.

As soon as he finished his meal, the lawyer took a candle and went to his study. There, he opened his safe and took out a document. The envelope read: "Dr. Jekyll's Will." The will was hand written by the respected doctor

himself, because Utterson had refused to let
the will be drafted by his clerk. He had been
too shocked by its contents when Jekyll first
approached him, and he was still shocked.
For friendship's sake only, he had consented
to be the guardian of the will and to present it
to the courts if it became necessary to do so.

With a sigh, the lawyer put on his specta-
cles and sat down to read once more the puzzling contents of the will insisted on by Jekyll.
The first part could, perhaps, be acceptable,
for a lawyer cannot dictate to whom a client
should leave his money. This part provided
that in the event of Jekyll's death, all his pos-
sessions were to pass into the hands of his
"friend and benefactor, Edward Hyde."

But the second part did not make any
sense to Utterson. It specified that in case of
the doctor's "disappearance or unexplained
absence for any period exceeding three calen-
dar months," Edward Hyde should step into

Reading the Will's Puzzling Contents

THE STRANGE CASE OF
DR. JEKYLL AND MR. HYDE

Henry Jekyll's shoes without further delay and be free from any obligation beyond the payment of a few small sums of money to the members of the doctor's household staff.

Mr. Utterson had never heard of such an arrangement, and he had practiced law for close to forty years. And tonight brought a new burden as he read the familiar pages. Tonight he learned something of the character of this Edward Hyde. Before, Hyde had just been a name in the will, but now he had become an actual living being... a fiend! Utterson replaced the will in his safe, wishing he could do something about the fanciful provisions Jekyll had made.

"Disappearance, indeed!" muttered the lawyer. Richard's suggestion of blackmail came to his mind, and he wondered if that could be true. "Is there some disgrace in store for Henry Jekyll that will force him to disappear?" he asked himself. Because Jekyll

A New Burden

was an old friend as well as a client, Utterson was quite upset by the story Richard had told him that morning. "Perhaps Lanyon can give me some insight into Henry's behavior," he decided.

Hastie Lanyon had been the third member of their trio at college: Jekyll, Lanyon, and Utterson—roommates and close friends. Lanyon was now a celebrated doctor.

Utterson blew out his candle and called to a servant for his overcoat. Then he walked the short distance to Lanyon's big house in Cavendish Square.

Dr. Lanyon was still at the dinner table, sitting alone over his wine. He was delighted to see Utterson and in his boisterous manner made him very welcome. Such liveliness in anyone else would have irritated a man as quiet as Utterson. But this friendship had been formed so long ago that the hearty, white-haired medical man was the one person

A Lively Welcome by Dr. Lanyon

Utterson trusted and liked above all other people. The lawyer accepted a glass of wine from his friend and settled into a comfortable chair.

"I suppose, Lanyon, that you and I must be the two oldest friends that Henry Jekyll has," began Utterson.

"I wish the friends were younger," said Lanyon with a laugh. "But what of that? I see little of Jekyll now."

"Indeed?" said Utterson, surprised. "I thought you two were especially close, since you are both medical men."

"We were," replied Lanyon. "But for almost ten years, Jekyll has become more and more fanciful. Too much so for me. He began to go wrong, wrong in mind."

Utterson sipped his wine, his uneasy feelings still with him. "How do you mean 'fanciful'?" he asked.

Lanyon suddenly lost his good mood. "Such

Discussing Henry Jekyll

unscientific nonsense he bothers with!" he exploded. "No friendship could withstand it."

Instantly Utterson was relieved, and he thought to himself, "Ah, they have differed on some point of science. There has been no unsavory personal reason to turn Lanyon against Jekyll." But wishing to make sure of his conclusion, Utterson waited until Lanyon had had some more wine to help him regain his composure. Then he ventured the question he had come to ask.

"Did you ever come across a good friend of Jekyll's—one Edward Hyde?" he asked.

"Hyde?" repeated Lanyon. "No. Never heard of him. After my time, I guess."

Utterson was somewhat calmed that no scandal had reached Lanyon's ears. So he finished his wine and left. He could not know this was the last time he would see his old friend Lanyon healthy, smiling, and able to bid him a cheery good-night.

A Cheery Good-Night

One Set of Dreams

CHAPTER 4

Mr. Hyde and Mr. Seek

After his visit to Dr. Lanyon, Mr. Utterson did not sleep well. He tossed and turned until three in the morning. When he finally slept, he dreamed and moaned. Over and over he saw snatches of pictures: a child running, a man walking very fast, a collision of the two, the child on the ground with the man's foot about to descend on her arm. A new set of pictures: Henry Jekyll asleep in his large and richly furnished bedroom, the embroidered curtains around the bed plucked apart by a hand with dirty, broken nails, Jekyll in a robe seated at

Brand START.

his desk, being forced to write a check for ninety pounds by a man standing over him.

The man in these two dreams haunted the lawyer all night and into the day. Yet the man had no face that Utterson could recognize, though he knew the man in his dream was Edward Hyde.

When he awoke in the morning, Mr. Utterson made a decision while the nightmares still had hold over him. He decided to see this Hyde for himself.

"Mysteries often vanish when facts are brought forward," reasoned Utterson, as he made plans. "So if I replace a phantom Hyde with the real Hyde, I might understand the reason for Jekyll's will. At least Hyde's face will be worth seeing for two reasons besides the will: It caused instant hatred in my cousin Richard, and its owner is without mercy toward children."

From that morning on, Mr. Utterson went

Another Set of Dreams

to the street of "Blackmail House" whenever he could free himself from his legal work. He would linger near the scarred door in the early morning, in the evening after dinner, and late into the night. With a wry smile, he said to himself, "If he is Mr. Hyde, then I shall be Mr. Seek."

At last, Utterson's patience was rewarded. It was a clear night with a touch of frost in the air. The shops near "Blackmail House" were closed, and the lawyer was the only person about in the small street. Near ten o'clock, Mr. Utterson became aware of an odd, light footstep. A tingling in his spine told him that the man he sought was approaching. Utterson stepped back into the courtyard next to the door just as a small, plainly dressed man crossed the street, stopped at the door, and took out a key.

Mr. Utterson came out of the gloom and said loudly, "Mr. Hyde, I think?"

Utterson Becomes "Mr. Seek."

Utterson Introduces Himself to Mr. Hyde.

CHAPTER 5

Will a Blackmailer Turn to Murder?

Mr. Hyde shrank back with a hissing intake of breath. But his fear was only temporary, for he answered coolly, "That is my name. What do you want?" He kept his head turned from the lawyer, though his eyes darted over Utterson's face in a sideways glance.

"I saw you were about to enter," answered Utterson. "I am an old friend of Dr. Jekyll, Gabriel John Utterson, the lawyer. I'm sure he has spoken of me. I am about to visit the doctor and I thought that you might admit me."

"Dr. Jekyll is not at home. How did you know me?" Hyde asked, still looking away.

"Let us exchange favors," Utterson suggested. "I will answer you if you will let me see your face."

Mr. Hyde hesitated. Then he turned and faced Utterson with an air of defiance. The two men stared at each other for several seconds before Utterson spoke.

"Now I shall know you again," he said. "It may be useful."

"Yes," agreed Hyde. "It is well that we have met. Also you should have my address." He named a street and number in Soho.

"Good God!" thought Utterson. "Has he, too, been thinking about the will?" But Utterson said nothing, merely nodding his head to indicate that he heard the address.

"Now," said Hyde, "how did you know me?"

"A description from common friends."

"Common friends?" echoed Hyde, a little

A Defiant Face!

hoarsely. "Who are they?"

"Jekyll, for instance," said Utterson.

"He never told you!" cried Hyde, with a flush of anger. "I did not expect that you would lie to me."

"Oh, now see here. That is not fitting language," said the lawyer mildly.

Hyde snarled aloud—a snarl that turned into a savage laugh. The next moment, with extraordinary quickness, he unlocked the door and disappeared into the house.

Mr. Utterson stood awhile where Hyde had left him, the picture of confusion and dissatisfaction. Then he turned and walked slowly up the street, his mind going over the scene again. Hyde was pale and dwarfish. He gave the impression of being deformed, yet his body did not have a specific defect. His smile was unpleasant, and his manner was disturbing, for he managed to be both timid and bold at the same time. The final point

Hyde Disappears into the House.

against him was his husky, whispering, and somewhat broken voice. But these objections did not account for the loathing and fear Utterson felt for Hyde.

"He is Satan himself!" Utterson cried to the night. "And this is the man Henry Jekyll has chosen to be his friend and heir."

Around the corner, Mr. Utterson entered a square of handsome old houses. Most were now shabby and broken up into small units, leased to anyone able to afford the low rent. However, one house, the second from the corner, was still occupied by one owner only. It had an air of wealth and comfort about it. Though only a hall light showed, Mr. Utterson knocked at its door. A well-dressed, sternfaced servant answered.

"Good evening, Poole," said the lawyer. "Is Dr. Jekyll at home?"

"I will see, Mr. Utterson," said Poole, opening the door wider so the lawyer could enter

"Is Dr. Jekyll At Home?"

Brandon Encl

the large hall. It was furnished with finely carved oak cabinets standing on a thick, dark red rug.

"Will you wait here by the fire, sir, or shall I give you a light in the dining room?" asked Poole, motioning toward the large, brightly burning fireplace.

"Here, thank you, " said the lawyer.

Utterson warmed himself by the fire until Poole returned with the announcement that Dr. Jekyll had gone out. Utterson sighed with relief at the butler's words, then felt ashamed of himself.

Casually he said, "I saw Mr. Hyde go into the house by the old dissecting room door, Poole. Does Dr. Jekyll allow that when he is not at home?"

"Yes, it's quite all right, sir," answered Poole. "Mr. Hyde has a key."

"Your master seems to trust that young man a great deal," continued the lawyer,

Utterson Warms Himself by the Fire.

making his comment almost a question.

"Yes, indeed, sir," replied Poole. "We all have orders to obey him."

Mr. Utterson turned to the door, then said as if in afterthought, "I don't remember meeting Mr. Hyde here at any of Dr. Jekyll's excellent dinners."

Poole was shocked. "Oh, no, sir. He never *dines* here. Indeed, we see little of him on this side of the house, in the living quarters. He mostly comes and goes by the laboratory."

"I see. Well, good-night, Poole."

"Good night, Mr. Utterson."

The lawyer walked home with a very heavy heart. "Poor Henry Jekyll," he thought. "I fear he is deeply involved with something wicked. It's true he was a wild young man during our college days, but that was so many years ago. Any sins he committed then should have been long forgiven and forgotten. But now someone seems to have dug up some

Utterson Questions Poole about Mr. Hyde.

secret and, I fear, is blackmailing him."

As Utterson reflected, it occurred to him that Hyde, himself, looked as if he had many old and new secret sins to conceal also, though he was actually a young man. One sin, at least, Utterson knew about from his cousin Richard—blackmail. But he feared an even worse crime was being planned—murder!

"There is great danger for Jekyll," thought Utterson. "For if that creature Hyde suspects the existence of Jekyll's leaving him everything, he may be so impatient to inherit it, he would hasten Jekyll's death."

Utterson entered his own door with a new determination. He would see Henry Jekyll. He would not let a calamity like this befall one of his oldest friends while he sat by, doing nothing. No, he would insist on helping Jekyll out of whatever trouble he was in. And together, he and Jekyll would break the hold Hyde had over the doctor.

Fearing a Worse Crime — Murder!

Dinner at Dr. Jekyll's

CHAPTER 6

Mr. Utterson's Promise

Mr. Utterson was invited to Henry Jekyll's for dinner a few days later. This was a good piece of luck, in view of his determination to help the doctor. There were five other old friends present, and the conversation was lively and intelligent, with appreciation for Jekyll's excellent food and wine.

When the others had gone, Mr. Utterson stayed behind. This had become a habit with himself and Jekyll after such dinners. It was pleasant to sit by the fire, chatting about the evening in a quiet way after the previous gaiety. Tonight, Utterson studied Henry Jekyll carefully, but saw no change in the man he had known for years.

Dr. Jekyll, though he had been close friends with Utterson and Lanyon at school, was younger than they, for he had been a prodigy, very advanced in his studies. Even now, the large, well-made, smooth-faced Jekyll looked much younger than his fifty years. His expression was kindly, with perhaps a slight suggestion of slyness. But now his face bore only a look of contentment and affection as he poured Mr. Utterson another glass of wine and they relaxed in comfortable chairs.

Mr. Utterson cleared his throat. "I have been wanting to speak with you, Jekyll. You know that will of yours?"

A tiny frown tugged at the doctor's smooth face, but he answered with humor. "My dear Utterson, you are unfortunate to have such a client as myself. I never saw anyone as

An After-Dinner Chat

distressed by a will as you are by mine. No, I take that back. I have seen Lanyon more distressed by my own scientific ideas—ideas which he calls my scientific heresies—my disagreement with accepted ideas. Now, don't frown. I know he's a good fellow, but he's also the most ignorant, stubborn man I've ever known. I have never been more disappointed in a man that I am in Lanyon."

Utterson refused to be switched over to this new topic. "You know, Jekyll, I never approved of your will. I said so from the first."

"Yes, certainly I know that," said Jekyll a trifle sharply. "You keep saying so."

"And I must say so again," said the lawyer, "because I have heard something abominable about young Hyde."

The large, handsome face of Jekyll grew pale to the very lips, and a blackness came about his eyes. "I don't wish to hear any more on this topic," he said firmly and coldly.

Jekyll Tries To Change the Topic.

"But..." began Utterson.

"No. Whatever you have heard can make no difference." Jekyll spoke rapidly and angrily. "My position is very strong And it cannot be changed by talk. So enough of this!"

"I want to help you," Utterson answered slowly and calmly. "You know I am to be trusted. Tell me in confidence, and I have no doubt but that I can rescue you."

With an effort, Jekyll regained his composure. "My dear friend, that is very good of you. I would trust you of all men, yes, even before myself, if I could make that choice. But the situation is not what you imagine. Nothing so bad, in fact. But it is a private matter. To set your mind at ease, I will say one thing—at any moment I choose, I can be rid of Mr. Hyde. I give you my word on that. But thank you again and again."

Utterson sighed. "No doubt you know best," he said as he rose. "And now it is getting late,

Rickey End 16 JAN 28

"I Want To Help You."

and I must be getting home."

By raising his hand, Jekyll made him pause. "Just one more thing before we put this topic from us forever," said Jekyll. "I have a great interest in poor Hyde. He told me you had seen him, and I fear he was rude. But, old friend, will you promise me something?"

"What?"

"If I am taken away, will you defend his rights for him, in spite of his manner, and see that he gets all I wish him to have? I think you would if you knew everything."

"I can't pretend that I shall ever like him," said the lawyer.

"I don't ask that," pleaded Jekyll, putting his hand on Utterson's arm. "I only ask for justice. I only ask you to help him for my sake...when I am no longer here."

Utterson nodded his head, but his face was terribly sad. "Very well, Jekyll," he said. "I promise."

"Help Him for My Sake."

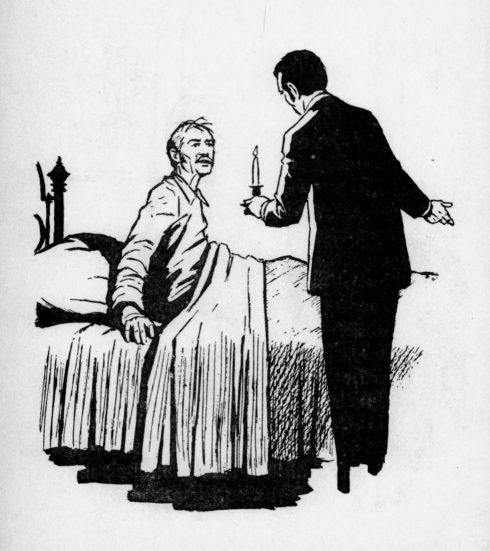

Utterson Is Awakened at Dawn.

CHAPTER 7

Witness to a Murder

A year passed uneventfully, and Utterson scolded himself many times over for his alarm over Mr. Hyde and Dr. Jekyll. Therefore, the visit of Inspector Newcomen came as a great shock to Uterson—greater than if he had continued to expect the worst news from Jekyll during that year.

One morning. just as dawn was breaking, Utterson's man servant woke him, saying a detective from Scotland Yard was downstairs and wished to talk to him most urgently.

The lawyer dressed hurriedly and rushed

downstairs to see what the detective wanted.

When Utterson entered the parlor, where his butler had asked the officers to wait, he was amazed to see an unknown young woman in a maid's uniform sitting on one of his antique chairs, weeping. A policeman stood behind her, while the man from Scotland Yard, Inspector Newcomen, was writing in a small notebook. The inspector apologized to Utterson for the intrusion and for the early hour. Then he drew the lawyer aside to explain the circumstances of their visit and the identity of the young woman.

"A terrible crime was committed just a few hours ago," said the inspector. "That girl is a housemaid, and she is the sole witness to it. We believe you can help us, so I wish you to hear the details of the crime from her own lips. Of course, you will make allowances for her shock at what she has seen."

Mr. Utterson nodded, and they turned

The Sole Witness to a Crime

back to the others. The girl wiped her eyes, which were large and blue. She seemed more frightened by her elegant surroundings than by the policeman at her side, for she crouched rather than sat in Mr. Utterson's expensive chair and did not touch its polished arms.

"Now, Sarah," said the inspector briskly, "here is Mr. Utterson, waiting to hear your story. No more tears, if you please."

Though her eyes had filled with tears again, Sarah choked back her sobs and said, "Yes, sir, I'll try, sir. I finished me duties and went to my room around eleven o'clock. Then, while I was sitting at me window and looking at the moon, I saw this fine old gentleman walking toward...."

Utterson interrupted. "You were looking at the moon, you say?"

Sarah flushed. "Yes, sir. The river is down below the house, and the moon looks ever so nice shining on it. It's like a picture in the

Sitting at the Window

storybooks I used to read at school."

The inspector snapped his fingers impatiently. "All right, get on with it. You saw the victim approach."

Sarah nodded, a few tears escaping from her eyes. "He looked ever so fine, and yet I could tell he was a kind gentleman from the way he smiled at Mr. Hyde."

"Mr. Hyde!" exclaimed Utterson.

"Oh, it was Mr. Hyde right enough," said Sarah. "I know him, for he sometimes calls at my master's house, and none of us servants likes him. So mean-looking and short-tempered, he is. We all try to avoid him."

Now the inspector broke in, for the story was getting confused. He explained to the lawyer that two men happened to meet across the road from where Sarah watched at her window. The older man was apparently asking for directions, for he pointed in one direction after bowing politely. The second

Two Men Met on the Road.

man was Hyde. The inspector ordered Sarah to resume her story.

"Mr. Hyde didn't answer him, that I could tell. He waved his big cane about and seemed to want the old gentleman out of the way. He stamped his feet, almost like he was taken by a fit.

"Well, sir, the old gentleman was surprised, and he stepped back. I guess he was a little afraid. I know I was, and I was safe indoors. But as soon as he stepped back, Mr. Hyde was on him! He lifted up that cane and brought it down ever so hard on the gentleman's head. He hit him and hit him. When the gentleman fell down, Mr. Hyde hit him some more. Then he jumped right on him, up and down. Just like them apes in the zoo do. That's when I left my senses."

"She had fainted," explained the inspector. "By the time she came to and called the police, it was two o'clock this morning. Mr. Hyde was

"He Jumped Right on Him, Up and Down."

gone, of course, but his victim lay in the road dead, horribly mangled. We found the bottom half of the cane in the gutter where it had rolled. It had been broken, even though it was made from some very tough and heavy wood. No doubt the murderer carried the top half away with him."

Mr. Utterson felt his legs tremble, and he sat down quickly. Dreading the answer, he asked, "Who was the victim?"

"We don't know yet," replied the inspector. "That's why we've come to you. The old man carried a purse and a gold watch, but no papers or cards of identity. But in his pocket was a stamped and sealed letter addressed to you. We assume he was looking for a post box and asked Hyde the location of one."

Mr. Utterson regained control of himself, and accompanied the group to the police station. There, the lawyer was led into a back room, where the body of the victim lay

A Letter Addressed to Utterson

beneath a rough prison blanket. When the blanket was pulled back from the face, Mr. Utterson gave a gasp.

"This is Sir Danvers Carew. He was a member of Parliament as well as a client of mine."

"Good God, sir!" exclaimed the inspector. "This killing will make a great deal of noise in the world. It is fortunate that we already know the name of the murderer. Now all we have to do is find him."

Utterson looked away from the corpse. "Perhaps I can help you there also," he said. "If he is the same Mr. Hyde that I am acquainted with, I have his address."

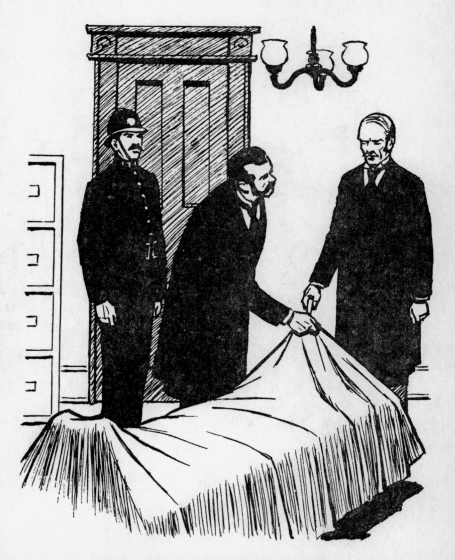

Utterson Identifies the Victim.

A Familiar Cane

CHAPTER 8

Where Is Mr. Hyde?

Before they left the police station, the inspector showed Mr. Utterson the murder weapon—the battered cane half taken from the gutter near the body. Now the lawyer had no doubts that the Hyde he knew was the one involved in this murder, for he recognized the cane as one he, himself, had given Henry Jekyll many years before.

The inspector hailed a cab, and the lawyer gave the driver directions to a street in Soho— that tumbled-down section of London which was home to thieves and murderers. It was now morning, but the first fog of the season had rolled in. The cab could only crawl through the infrequent patches of light. Utterson shuddered as he caught glimpses of the evil population of Soho through the swirling mists.

The cab let them off in front of a rooming house on a dirty street, where ragged children huddled in doorways and adults of many nationalities walked with a drunken sway. On one side was a gin shop, and on the other a cheap restaurant whose odors should have warned off customers.

Utterson and the inspector climbed the crumbling steps to Hyde's rooming house. Utterson felt slightly dazed.

"So this is the home of Henry Jekyll's best friend, the home of an heir to a quarter of a million pounds," thought Utterson.

The landlady, furious at being disturbed, screamed a curse as she opened the door. When she saw two men of quality, she manufactured a false smile of welcome.

The Cab Arrives in Dangerous Soho.

THE STRANGE CASE OF
DR. JEKYLL AND MR. HYDE

The inspector took charge, demanding to know Hyde's whereabouts, but the landlady said he was out.

"He came in very late last night, sir, and left again soon after," she explained. "But this wasn't odd, sir, for his habits were always irregular." She gave this information freely, but balked when the inspector asked to be let into Hyde's rooms.

Now Utterson spoke for the first time. "See here, woman, I better tell you who this person is you are refusing. He is Inspector Newcomen of Scotland Yard."

The woman gave a screech of joy. "Ahh, Hyde is in trouble! What's he done?"

Not replying, the two men exchanged a glance. "Hyde is as popular here as he is everywhere else," observed Newcomen.

Knowing now who her visitors were, the woman showed them at once to Hyde's rooms.

Here a surprise awaited, for the rooms

Hyde's Landlady Is Free with Information.

were furnished with luxury and good taste. There were damask napkins, silverware, and a closet filled with wine. Deep-piled rugs and several paintings would have even fitted well in Mr. Utterson's own house. He wondered if the paintings were a gift from Jekyll, who was an art collector.

But the rooms had been ransacked: Drawers stood open, clothes lay on the floor, and a pile of ashes on the hearth testified to the burning of many papers.

The inspector began his search. From the fireplace he fished out the stub end of a green checkbook, which was only charred. Behind a door he found the top half of the cane—the murder weapon This was the proof that Hyde was the wanted man.

The inspector and Utterson proceeded to the bank named on the charred checkbook. There, they found several thousand pounds in Hyde's account. The inspector's good humor

A Charred Checkbook and a Broken Cane

and confidence increased at this news.

"Now, sir," he told Utterson, "we have him almost in our hands. He left in a panic, or he wouldn't have burned his checkbook and forgotten the cane. He'll need the money he has on deposit. We'll circulate pictures of him, and the bank will alert us when he arrives."

This confidence was soon found to be misplaced. There were no photographs of Hyde, and his family could not be traced.

When an artist tried to compose a likeness of Hyde from the descriptions of his landlady and Sarah and a few others, the attempt was a failure. As often happens, their descriptions differed too widely. The one point they all agreed on was of no help to the artist—that point was Hyde's haunting impression of deformity without actually showing one.

Scotland Yard now redoubled its efforts in the search for Mr. Edward Hyde, the murderer of Sir Danvers Carew.

An Artist Tries To Compose a Likeness.

Poole Leads Utterson across the Yard.

CHAPTER 9

The Letter

It wasn't until late afternoon on the day of the murder of Sir Danvers Carew that Utterson could get away from the inspector and all the legal details concerning the death of his client. The lawyer hurried to Dr. Jekyll's home, where Poole greeted him, then led him through the house, out the back, and across the yard.

Utterson remembered that the previous owner of the house had been a prominent surgeon, who used to hold classes in his laboratory and dissecting rooms. It was toward these rooms that Poole was now leading the lawyer. At that time, the yard had been a garden, far different from the dismal emptiness it now was.

When they reached the laboratory and dissecting rooms, Utterson realized that he had never been in this part of Jekyll's quarters before. He eyed the tables crowded with chemical apparatus curiously. The floor was littered with open crates, the packing straw still strewn about. A short flight of stairs led from the laboratory to Jekyll's office.

Poole knocked, then opened the door. The office was a large room with three iron-barred dusty windows looking out onto the court. Its furnishings were usual for a doctor's office, except for a full-length mirror in one corner.

Because the fog still lay thickly over London, lamps had been lit. A fire burned in the grate, and huddled close beside it was Dr. Jekyll. He looked deathly sick and did not

At the Door to Jekyll's Office

rise to meet Utterson. But he held out a cold hand and welcomed him in a changed voice, as if it hurt him to speak.

As soon as Poole had left them, Utterson asked, "You have heard the news?"

Jekyll shuddered. "The newsboys were crying it in the square."

Utterson assumed a businesslike manner, so his words would be taken as coming from a lawyer, not a friend. "Carew was my client, Jekyll, but so are you, and I want to know what I am doing. You have not been mad enough to hide this fellow, have you?"

"Utterson, I swear I will never set eyes on him again!" cried Jekyll. "On my honor, I am done with him in this world! It is all at an end, believe me." Jekyll had risen and now stood before Utterson, waving his hands in a distracted way. "And indeed, the man is safe. He is quite safe and does not want my help. You do not know him as I do. Hear what I

Jekyll Has Heard the News.

say—he will never be heard of again."

The lawyer listened gloomily. He did not like Jekyll's feverish manner. "You seem pretty sure of him," he said slowly, "and for your sake, I hope you may be right. If it came to a trial, your name might appear. It would be scandalous."

"Oh, yes, yes, I am sure he is gone," exclaimed Jekyll. "*Why* I am sure, I cannot tell anyone." He paused and then resumed in a calmer tone. "However, I do need your advice on one thing. I have received a letter, and I don't know whether to show it to the police or not."

Utterson's usually impassive face took on an expression of interest. "From Hyde?"

Jekyll nodded.

"And you fear that it might lead to his capture?"

"No," replied Jekyll coolly. "I cannot say that I care what becomes of Hyde. I am only

"I Am Sure He Is Gone."

concerned for my own reputation. So I want to leave it all in your hands. I have the greatest trust in your judgement and I know you will act wisely."

Utterson thought it over. He was surprised at Jekyll's selfish view of the matter, but also relieved by it. "Very well," he said at last. "Let me see the letter."

The letter Jekyll handed to Utterson was written in an odd, upright hand and was signed "Edward Hyde." It was brief, saying that Dr. Jekyll, from whom the writer had received so much generosity and been unworthy of it, should not worry about the writer's safety, as he had a means of escape on which he could depend absolutely.

Utterson seemed relieved by the letter. It did not read like the letter of a blackmailer to his victim. With a nod of approval, he asked, "Where is the envelope?"

"I burned it before I realized that perhaps

A Letter from Edward Hyde

I should not have," replied Jekyll. "However, it bore no postmark, for it was delivered by messenger."

"Well, let me keep the letter and think over what to do," said Utterson.

"Thank you, thank you!" said Jekyll with relief. "I want you to make all decisions for me. I have lost confidence in myself."

"Tell me one thing," said the lawyer, with a return to sharpness. "It was Hyde who dictated the terms in your will about your disappearance, wasn't it?"

The doctor turned pale, and for a moment he seemed to sway in faintness. Then he nodded, his mouth tightly shut.

"I knew it!" cried Utterson. "He meant to murder you. You have had a narrow escape."

"Better than that," replied Jekyll solemnly, "I have had a lesson. Oh, God, Utterson, what a lesson I have had!" With that, Jekyll broke down and covered his face with his hands.

"Oh, God, What a Lesson I Have Had!"

THE STRANGE CASE OF
DR. JEKYLL AND MR. HYDE

When Jekyll finally quieted down, Utterson gave him an encouraging pat on the shoulder and left by the way he had come. He did not wish to use the scarred laboratory door though it was the nearer way out, for it was the very door at which he had stood watch for so many nights, hoping to see Hyde enter with his key.

Poole held the polished front door open for the lawyer s departure. saying, "Good afternoon, Mr. Utterson."

Utterson turned back to Poole for a moment. "A letter was delivered here today by messenger. Tell me, Poole, what did the messenger look like?"

Poole shook his head. "No, sir, you are mistaken. I, myself, handle all the mail. In the regular post today, there were only circulars from tradesmen. And there has been no letter delivered by a messenger. Of this I am certain."

No Letter Was Delivered.

Utterson Selects a Good Wine.

CHAPTER 10

A Comparison of Handwritings

As Mr. Utterson walked slowly home, his thoughts were on the letter he was carrying. Since Poole had not taken it in, it must have been delivered at the laboratory door. It was even possible that Hyde had written the letter in the doctor's office, since he had a key.

What troubled Utterson the most was how reliable was the letter. So he decided to talk to a person whose opinions he trusted—Mr. Guest, his chief clerk and longtime employee.

After ordering the fire built up in his study, Mr. Utterson descended to his cellar and selected a bottle of wine of a particularly good year. Then he invited Mr. Guest in for a chat and filled two glasses.

Mr. Guest was not only intelligent, but he was also interested in odd pastimes like the analysis of handwriting. Mr. Utterson had decided to show him Hyde's letter in the hope that some comment by Mr. Guest on the handwriting would help him to determine a course of action.

Utterson's clerk had known Dr. Jekyll for years, and, no doubt, had heard about Hyde's freedom of his house. Utterson kept no secrets from Mr. Guest, largely because the clerk never gossiped about any information that came his way through business dealings or just through his own acute observation.

Though Mr. Guest was some years younger than his employer, he was as quiet and dry as Utterson, and also appreciative of fine wine. Now the two men sat in silence for several minutes, sipping from their crystal glasses.

Inviting Mr. Guest In for a Chat

Mr. Guest rolled the wine on his tongue before swallowing. He smiled. "Ah, Mr. Utterson, sir, I have tasted many fine vintages from your cellar, but this one, I believe, surpasses them all."

"Yes, I think I would agree, Mr. Guest." Utterson let a few moments pass in which to savor the wine before he said, "This business about Sir Danvers is sad—quite sad for us as well as for Parliament."

"Yes, sir. The public is quite enraged at the brutality of the crime, especially against a Member of Parliament. The murderer must be a madman."

Mr. Utterson leaned forward and spoke in an even lower voice than usual. "I should like to have your views on that after you have looked over this document. It is a letter in the murderer's own handwriting, and I am undecided as to what to do about it."

"Indeed, sir? A document in the murderer's

Asking Guest's Views on Hyde's Letter

own handwriting? How very interesting." Mr. Guest allowed a note of excitement to creep into his voice, or perhaps it was the glow of the excellent wine cleverly provided by Utterson in the hopes of gaining his clerk's complete cooperation.

Mr. Utterson handed the letter to Mr. Guest. "This document is, of course, completely confidential."

Mr. Guest immediately put down his wine and studied the letter with intensity. "I would say this man is not mad. Still, he writes with a very odd hand."

Just then, a servant entered with a note. Mr. Utterson read it and dropped it on the table, where it caught Mr. Guest's eye.

"Is that note from Dr. Jekyll, sir?" he asked. Mr. Utterson nodded. "I thought I recognized the writing," continued Mr. Guest. "Is it a private communication, Mr. Utterson?"

A Servant Brings Utterson a Note.

"No, just an invitation to dinner. Why? Do you want to see it?"

"Just for a moment," said Mr. Guest as he picked up the invitation and held it beside the letter. He studied the two, nodding his head several times as he seemed to find points common to both. At last, he returned both documents to Utterson. "Thank you, sir. I am finished with them."

There was silence. Mr. Utterson realized his clerk was running true to form, keeping any secret to himself. So he slapped his hand on the back of the clerk's chair and said, "Well, Guest, out with it! Why did you compare the two? What have you found out?"

Mr. Guest replied dutifully, "Well, sir, there's a very interesting resemblance. In many points the two handwritings are exactly the same, except the letters slope differently."

"*Identical* except for **the** slant of the letters?" cried Utterson in amazement.

Guest Studies the Two Letters.

"Yes, sir," said Guest, picking up his glass again.

But Mr. Utterson had lost his taste for the wine. "This is, I repeat, a confidential matter, Guest," he said quietly.

His clerk nodded. "I understand, sir." Then he rose to return to his office.

As soon as Utterson had heard Guest's views on the handwriting in the two documents, his mind was made up. And the moment the door closed behind Guest, Utterson locked the so-called Hyde letter away in his safe, never to take it out and look at it again. As he slammed the safe door, he decided, "The world must not know that Henry Jekyll—my client and dear friend—has forged a letter for a vicious murderer in order to throw the police off his trail!"

Locking the Hyde Letter in the Safe

Dr. Jekyll Comes Out of Seclusion.

CHAPTER 11

Dr. Lanyon's Secret

In spite of a reward of several thousand pounds, Mr. Hyde was not captured. Information came daily to the police of his disreputable life and of his cruelty and violence, but not of his whereabouts. Privately, Mr. Utterson felt that the death of Sir Danvers was almost a fair exchange for the disappearance of so evil a man as Hyde.

Now that the dark influence of Hyde had ceased, Dr. Jekyll began a new life. He came out of seclusion and was once more a regular guest or host to his friends at delightful dinners. He redoubled his previous charity work with the poor and became prominent in church activities. Even his appearance changed to a more open and brighter look. This lasted for two months, during which time Utterson saw Henry Jekyll almost daily.

Then one day Utterson knew something was wrong. He came to call on Dr. Jekyll, but Poole answered his knock with the news that the doctor was at home but not seeing anyone. The same thing happened the next day and the next. Poole admitted that the doctor was not ill, but had left orders not to disturb him. All of Jekyll's charitable works stopped suddenly, along with his church work. He saw no one and went no place.

Utterson, by now very agitated by Jekyll's actions, decided to consult Dr. Lanyon about them, both as a friend and as a medical man. But he found Lanyon in a terrible condition himself.

"The Doctor Is Not Seeing Anyone."

THE STRANGE CASE OF
DR. JEKYLL AND MR. HYDE

Dr. Lanyon's large frame had shrunk, his rosy face turned pale, and a frightened quality had entered his manner. Utterson realized that Lanyon was a dying man.

The doctor confirmed Utterson's thoughts by nodding his head slowly. "I have had a shock from which I shall never recover. I used to enjoy life. Now I think that if we knew all, we would be glad to die."

"Jekyll is ill too—mentally, that is," said Utterson. "Have you seen him?" He knew that the two men had straightened out their differences and had resumed their friendship during these last two months. Lanyon held up a trembling hand.

"I wish to hear and see no more of Henry Jekyll," he cried. "I regard him as dead!"

"Come now, Lanyon," said Utterson softly. "We three are old friends. We shall not live long enough to make other friends."

"Nothing can be done," replied the dying

Dr. Lanyon Is Dying.

man. "Ask Jekyll for yourself."

Utterson shrugged. "He won't see me."

"That does not surprise me," said Lanyon. "Some day, Utterson, after I am dead, you may perhaps understand what all this is about. I cannot tell you. Now, stay and talk to me of anything except Henry Jekyll."

Utterson spent several hours with his old friend, but as soon as he got home, he wrote to Jekyll, asking why he was not permitted to visit and what he could do to mend the break between Jekyll and Lanyon.

The next day brought a strange answer. The letter was long, often pathetic, and sometimes darkly mysterious. It stated that the quarrel with Lanyon was permanent. As to his seclusion, Jekyll wrote: "You must not doubt my friendship if my door is often shut even to you. I have brought on myself a punishment and danger that I cannot name. If I am the chief of sinners, I am the chief of

A Mysterious Letter from Jekyll

sufferers too. Leave me alone, old friend. I must go my own dark way."

Utterson hardly knew what to make of this plea. With the evil influence of Hyde gone, Jekyll had become his old self. Now, that life of good deeds and friendship was once again cast aside. Was this madness?...Utterson did not know how else to explain it, but somehow he felt that Lanyon knew the answer.

Lanyon died within a few days of Utterson's visit. On the day after his burial, Utterson opened an envelope that Lanyon had left for him. The front read: "Private. For the eyes of G. J. Utterson, *alone*. To be opened after the death of H. Lanyon."

From the envelope, the lawyer drew another one. This was sealed, and Lanyon had written on it: "Not to be opened until the death or disappearance of Henry Jekyll."

Utterson gasped. There was that word "disappearance" again, just as in Jekyll's will.

Dr. Lanyon Is Buried.

But in the will, it had been written at the sinister suggestion of Mr. Hyde. What coincidence had caused it to appear on this document from Lanyon? The lawyer was very open the envelope at once but his honor and ethics stopped him. With a sigh he put the letter far back in his safe.

Utterson continued to call on Jekyll but had to be satisfied by reports of him from Poole. The doctor was now a recluse and stayed most of the time in his office in the laboratory. He often slept there, and he spoke to no one.

After a while, with Poole's reports so much the same every day, Utterson stopped calling on Dr. Jekyll. He could not help a man he was not permitted to see.

Tempted To Open the Sealed Envelope

Passing By "Blackmail House"

CHAPTER 12

Conversation at a Window

Mr. Utterson continued to walk on Sundays with his cousin Richard Enfield. On one stroll, they chanced to be in the street where Richard had once pointed out a door. When they came opposite "Blackmail House," they stopped and gazed at it.

"Well," said Richard, "that story's at an end. We'll never see Mr. Hyde again."

"I hope not," said Utterson. "Did I tell you I met him some months ago and shared your disgust?"

"It would be impossible to see Hyde and not

feel repulsion. By the way, Cousin, I finally realized that this door is a back way into the house of Dr. Henry Jekyll."

"Ah, poor Jekyll," said Mr. Utterson, his face clouded. "I am very uneasy about him. His butler tells me he spends most of his time back here in his office. I wonder if... Come, Richard, let's cross the street."

Always agreeable, Richard followed his cousin into the cool, slightly damp courtyard. Mr. Utterson halted under the barred windows of the upper floor and looked up. A figure was sitting beside one window, which was open.

"Aha!" said Utterson, smiling with great satisfaction as he waved and called out, "Jekyll, is that you?"

Dr. Jekyll looked down, his face filled with sadness. He had been taking the air at the barred window like a prisoner. Recognizing Utterson, he lifted a hand weakly in greeting.

"I trust you are better," said Utterson.

Utterson Spies Jekyll at the Window.

"I am very weak, Utterson," replied Jekyll drearily, "very weak. It will not last long, thank God." His voice was very faint.

"You stay indoors too much," said the lawyer. "You need to whip up a little circulation. By the way, this is my cousin, Richard Enfield. Richard, Dr. Jekyll."

Richard bowed. "How do you do, sir?" he called pleasantly. "My cousin is right. Won't you come out with us? A hat is all you need."

A long, pained sigh drifted down. "Thank you, sir. I should like to very much, but it is impossible. I dare not." Jekyll made a visible attempt to straighten his shoulders and rouse himself in general. "But, indeed, Utterson, I am very glad to see you. I would invite you and Mr. Enfield up, but the office is really not fit to entertain in."

"Why, then," returned Utterson cheerfully, "we will stay down here and have our conversation from where we are."

"I Am Very Weak."

A sad smile touched the doctor's lips. "That is just what I was going to suggest."

The words were hardly spoken when the smile was wiped from his face. It was followed by an expression of such complete terror and despair that the two men below gasped. They saw the terrible look for just a second, then Jekyll slammed down the window and disappeared from their view.

Utterson and Richard stood frozen. Then, as one, they turned and left the courtyard in silence. Mr. Utterson's shoulders sagged as they walked on, away from the scarred door. Richard, though as pale as his cousin, was younger and stronger, and he slipped a steadying hand under the lawyer's elbow. But neither spoke. There was nothing to be said.

Jekyll Slams Down the Window.

Poole Enters the Parlor.

CHAPTER 13

The Search for a Mysterious Drug

After dinner one evening, Mr. Utterson was reading when his butler entered to say that Poole was in the hall, asking to speak with him most urgently.

"Show him in, of course," said the lawyer. Poole entered the parlor, his face pale and his body trembling.

"Bless me, Poole!" said Mr. Utterson. "What's the matter? You look ill. Or is the doctor ill? Come closer to the fire."

"Mr. Utterson," cried Poole, "there is something very wrong!"

"First calm yourself," said the lawyer. "Sit down. Here is a glass of wine. Then take your time and tell me what the trouble is." Utterson was long used to handling agitated clients.

Poole obeyed him. "You know the doctor's ways, Mr. Utterson, sir. How he keeps to his office. Shuts himself completely away, he does. And now I'm afraid, and that's the truth of it."

"Afraid?" asked Utterson. "Of what?" Poole ignored the question. "I've been afraid for a week now." His voice rose. "I can't bear it any longer. None of us can."

Utterson spoke a little sharply. "Poole, tell me exactly what you fear."

Poole raised frightened eyes to the lawyer's questioning ones. "Foul play, Mr. Utterson. I think there's been foul play."

Utterson could get no details from the usually calm, controlled, clear-thinking butler. The man was now so terrified, all he could do

Poole Fears Foul Play.

was plead that Utterson should come and see for himself. At once, Utterson called for his hat and coat, noticing the relief that swept Poole's face as he did so.

It was a wild, cold night in March. The moon was pale, lying on its back, as if the wind had tilted it. The wind made talking difficult, so Poole said nothing more, and Mr. Utterson remained unprepared for what he had to face. But the anticipation of disaster made him hurry.

Poole knocked softly at Jekyll's front door. The door opened, but a chain was still fastened. A woman's voice asked, "Is that you, Poole?"

"That's right. Open the door."

They entered a brightly lit hall with a fire roaring in the grate. A huddled group of people turned anxious faces toward them, and Utterson saw they were Jekyll's servants. A housemaid was weeping uncontrollably. And

Hurrying Through a Wild, Cold Night

Jekyll's cook ran to him, clasping her hands and crying, "Bless God! It's Mr. Utterson come to help us."

"What is all this?" demanded the lawyer. "Why are you idling in the hall?"

Poole spoke up for all. "We're afraid," he said. Then taking a candle, he added, "Please, sir, follow me to the laboratory. Make no noise, but just listen. And if Dr. Jekyll should want to see you, *don't go in.*"

Though amazed at this advice, Utterson did not comment. He quietly followed Poole up the stairs to the office.

Poole knocked, saying, "Sir, Mr. Utterson is asking to see you." He cautioned the lawyer to listen by raising his hand to his ear.

A voice from within the office said, "Tell him I cannot see anyone."

"Thank you, sir," replied Poole, and they hastily retraced their steps. "Now, Mr. Utterson, was that my master's voice?"

The Servants Are Frightened.

Utterson hesitated. "It's...changed."

"Changed! I should think so!" cried Poole. "My master is dead! But who is in that office pretending to be Dr. Jekyll? Him that murdered him eight days ago! We heard the master cry out then, calling upon God. After that, this strange voice started answering to my knock and giving out orders."

Mr. Utterson wiped his forehead, for anxiety was making him perspire. "This is a wild tale you're telling me, Poole. Why would a murderer remain behind after he's done his killing? It's not reasonable."

"I can answer that, sir," said Poole. "Him or it or whatever is living now in that office has been demanding some special medicine night and day. Dr. Jekyll always had a habit of writing out orders to the chemists and throwing the paper out on the stairs for me. Well, this past week there's been nothing but sheets of paper and me running back and

"Who Is in That Office?"

forth to different wholesale chemists."

Utterson shrugged. "An important experiment must be in the making. There's nothing odd about that, is there?"

"Wait, sir, I haven't finished. None of these medicines I bring back is the right one. Soon there's another paper to another chemist, along with an order to return the drug I just brought home. This medicine is wanted most urgently as you can see."

"Have you any of these papers?" asked Utterson.

Poole searched his pockets and brought out a crumpled sheet. Bending closer to the candle, Mr. Utterson read: "Dr. Jekyll presents his compliments to Messrs. Maw, Chemists. I wish to inform you that your last sample was impure. Two years ago I purchased a large quantity of this same drug, and I desire the same good quality as I received then. Please search your warehouse for more of that same

Utterson Reads Jekyll's Letter.

lot. Expense is no object."

Up to this point, the letter was very carefully written and in a professional tone. But now the writer's emotions spilled over, for the handwriting became unsteady and the words read: "For God's sake, find me some of the old!"

Mr. Utterson looked up from the paper. "This is most disturbing. But the letter is not sealed. Are you daring to open his letters?"

"Oh, no, sir. I delivered it sealed, but the man at Maw's got angry when he read it and threw it back at me like so much dirt. He said Dr. Jekyll was to stop bothering them, for they had sent their best to him and were not used to having it rejected."

The lawyer looked harder at the paper in his hand. "I would say that this letter was unquestionably written by Dr. Jekyll. Do you deny this, Poole?"

Poole sighed. "No, sir. It does seem very

The Chemist Got Angry at Poole.

like his hand. But now I must tell you the worst part—I have seen this person—*this thing*—in the office. It slipped out to dig among the crates in the laboratory just as I came in through the garden entrance."

Mr. Utterson was very still. "I'm listening, Poole."

"He looked up when I came in and gave a funny kind of cry. Then he whipped right up the stairs and back into the office. He slammed the door something awful." Poole's voice lowered, a note of horror creeping into it. "Why would my master have covered his face from me? Why would he have cried out like a rat and run from me?" Poole threw out his hands in a show of bewilderment.

Mr. Utterson tried to hang onto common sense logic, which a lawyer was trained to do. "I grant you these are odd circumstances, Poole. But it must be that Dr. Jekyll has fallen in with a sickness that has tortured and

"Why Would He Have Run from Me?"

deformed him. That is the reason for covering his face, for the strangeness of his voice, for his avoidance of his friends. And, of course, he is desperately searching for a cure, so sends you from chemist to chemist. All this is natural to my way of thinking."

Now Poole drew himself up and spoke out firmly, almost defiantly, with none of his usual humility or politeness. "No, sir, I say not! What I saw was a dwarf, not the tall, fine person of my master. That *thing is* not Dr. Jekyll! How could it be? No, I tell you Dr. Jekyll has been murdered! To that I'll swear!"

For two long minutes Utterson thought it over. Finally he said, "Poole, if your belief is that strong, there is only one thing to do. We must go back into the house and get some tools, then break down the door to the office!"

"That *Thing* Is Not Dr. Jekyll!"

Poole Gives Utterson a Poker.

CHAPTER 14

The Dead Man

"That's it, Mr. Utterson!" exclaimed Poole. "Just what I hoped you'd say!"

"I'll see to it, Poole, that I bear full responsibility for this action. What have you got around here that we can use on the door?"

"There's an axe in the laboratory, sir. We use it to open crates. And here's a heavy poker for you." Poole selected one of the fireplace tools and handed it to the lawyer.

Mr. Utterson felt its weight. "A good piece of iron," he observed. "I hope I will not need such protection, but I think we both know more than we've said."

"Yes, sir, that's the way of it."

"Then let us make a clean breast of the matter. You recognized that figure even though he had his face covered?"

Poole did not hesitate. "I admit it moved quickly out of my view and was so doubled up that another man might not recognize him. But I *know* that it was Mr. Hyde. We never got back his key to the laboratory door. Besides—did you ever meet Mr. Hyde, sir?"

"Yes," said the lawyer, "once."

"Then you'll know as how there's something very queer about him. It gives you a scare just to see him."

"I admit I felt something like that."

"Well, sir, when this monkeylike creature jumped and ran off into the office, a feeling like ice went down my spine. That's what makes me sure it was Mr. Hyde."

"It's as I feared all along. Poor Henry has been murdered for his money." Utterson

Fearing That Jekyll Has Been Murdered

looked at the servants still huddled on the other side of the hall, pointed at one, and said to Poole, "Call that man over."

A big footman answered Poole's summons. In spite of his large size, he was pale and nervous. But he listened intelligently to Mr. Utterson's instructions—he was to arm himself and one of the bigger kitchen boys with heavy pokers. They were to stand in the street and guard the scarred door in case the *thing* tried to escape that way or was able to overpower both Poole and Utterson.

"I will give you ten minutes to arm yourselves and take up your post, " said the lawyer.

After the servants left, Utterson motioned Poole to follow him. They crept to the laboratory, where Poole located an axe. Consulting his watch, Mr. Utterson signalled that it was not yet time—it was not yet ten minutes. They could hear footsteps inside the office, going back and forth, back and forth.

Instructions for the Footman

THE STRANGE CASE OF
DR. JEKYLL AND MR. HYDE

"That's the way it walks all day, sir," whispered Poole, "and sometimes all the night. Stops only when a new chemist's sample is delivered, and then just for a short time. Tell me, sir, do they sound at all like the doctor's footsteps?"

The steps fell lightly and oddly, with a certain swing, though they went slowly. They were much different from the heavy tread of Henry Jekyll. Utterson shook his head and said, "No, they do not."

"Once, " said Poole, "I heard it weeping."

"Weeping?" said Utterson with a sudden chill of horror.

"True, sir. It was enough to make me want to join in. Like a lost soul, it was."

The ten minutes allowed the footman and kitchen boy were up. Poole set the candle on a nearby table, and he and Utterson mounted the stairs. The footsteps in the office still sounded in the silence, but at Utterson's

Ready To Mount the Stairs

words, they came to an abrupt halt.

"Jekyll!" cried Utterson in a loud voice. "I demand to see you! "

There was only silence.

"I warn you," continued the lawyer. "Our suspicions are aroused. I intend to see you, even if we have to break down the door so I can do so."

"Utterson!" cried the voice from within. "For God's sake, have mercy!"

"That's not Jekyll's voice," said the lawyer. "It's Hyde's! Down with the door, Poole!" He stepped back so Poole would have room in which to swing the axe.

The first blow shook the whole laboratory, but only splintered the wood beside the lock. A dismal screech rang out from the office. It was like an animal's terror. Up went the axe again. And down. One of the panels opened. But the door, like everything in Henry Jekyll's house, was strongly built, so it was

Poole Swings.

not until the fifth blow that the lock finally burst and the wrecked door fell inward.

A moment of quiet followed the loud blows and the crash of the door. Mr. Utterson peered into the office and saw a good fire going and the kettle on for tea. On a table, a delicate porcelain teapot waited for the kettle. On another table, papers were neatly stacked with a few bottles of chemicals in a row. Only one was out of line.

Mr. Utterson slowly made his way into this quiet, comfortable room and looked around carefully. Behind a large chair, he spotted a foot. It belonged to a man lying face down on the floor. Utterson reached down and turned the figure over.

Poole, right behind the lawyer, drew in his breath. "I was right!" he cried. "It's Mr. Hyde!"

"Yes," said Mr. Utterson, "and he is dead!"

Finding Mr. Hyde Dead!

Searching For Dr. Jekyll's Body

CHAPTER 15

Dr. Jekyll Disappears

The dead man was dressed in clothes far too large for him. Poole pointed out that he was wearing a favorite cashmere jacket of Dr. Jekyll's. In one hand, Hyde was clutching a broken glass tube, and the scent of bitter almonds was in the air.

"A suicide," pronounced Mr. Utterson. "We have come too late either to save him or to punish him. Now the only thing we can do, Poole, is find the body of your master."

With great energy, they searched the office, its closets and corners. Finding no one, they extended the search into the laboratory.

There, most closets were empty or screened with undisturbed, dusty cobwebs, so it was apparent that no body could have been stuffed in recently.

"He might be buried under the flooring," suggested Poole without much conviction. "Or maybe he was taken out the back door and buried elsewhere." But when they examined the back door, they found it locked and the key thrown in a corner, broken and rusted. Baffled, they returned to the office.

Mr. Utterson began a methodical search of the room, not for a body, but for a clue. He glanced at a book lying open on the tea table. It was a religious work that Jekyll had once praised to him. Now Utterson saw blasphemies—wild, raging criticisms—written by Jekyll on its pages. The lawyer turned away, upset, and saw Poole wiping a smudge of dirt from his face at the full-length mirror.

"I was just thinking, Mr. Utterson," said

A Broken and Rusted Key

Poole. "If this looking glass could only talk, it would tell us what we want to know."

Utterson nodded in agreement. "No doubt it has seen some strange sights here. And no sight more strange than its own presence in a room of science. I wonder why Jekyll installed it."

Poole had no answer as he adjusted his tie. Utterson turned to the orderly stacks of papers on one table and found an envelope addressed to himself on top. When he opened it, three documents fell out.

The first was a will by Jekyll, drawn up in the same eccentric terms as the one locked away in the lawyer's safe. But where Hyde's name appeared in the original will in Utterson's safe, in this new will, Utterson's own name had been substituted.

"Bless me, what can this mean?" exclaimed the lawyer. "Jekyll cut Hyde out of his will in my favor, yet Hyde did not destroy the will!

An Envelope Addressed to Utterson

THE STRANGE CASE OF
DR. JEKYLL AND MR. HYDE

He surely had no cause to like me."

The next document brought a cry of joy from Utterson because it was marked with the date. "Oh, Poole!" cried the lawyer. "Look here. Dr. Jekyll was alive and in this room today. Hyde could not have disposed of him so quickly. He must be alive and in hiding."

Poole's excitement turned to puzzlement. "Why should he hide, Mr. Utterson?"

"Ah, that is the point, Poole. Am I correct in calling this man on the floor a suicide? We must proceed very carefully in order not to involve the doctor in some catastrophe. Listen to what he writes."

Utterson read aloud: "My dear Utterson: When this shall fall into your hands, I shall have disappeared. How or why I shall have gone, I cannot foresee. But I feel the end is near. Lanyon told me he intended to place a document in your hands. Read it now. Then if you wish to know more, turn to the confession

"He Must Be Alive and In Hiding."

I have enclosed with this letter. I am your unworthy and unhappy friend, Henry Jekyll."

The two men stared down at the table at the sealed packet that was Jekyll's confession. Finally the lawyer picked it up and put it in his pocket.

"I am going home, Poole, where I can read this document in quiet," said Utterson. "But first I will read Dr. Lanyon's document, which is in my safe. Whether Dr. Jekyll is in hiding or is dead, we can at least try to save his reputation." He consulted his watch. "It is now ten o'clock. I will be back before midnight, and we will send for the police at that time."

Poole nodded and followed Utterson out of the office and the laboratory, locking the door to the laboratory after them. Although Poole had removed the kettle from the fireplace in the doctor's office, the fire continued to burn brightly, keeping a dead man warm.

Henry Jekyll's Confession

Time To Read Lanyon's Letter

CHAPTER 16

A Midnight Visitor

On returning home, Mr. Utterson went immediately to his safe. He took out the document sent to him by Dr. Lanyon before his death. Throwing off his coat and sitting himself in an armchair, he looked at the first page. The handwriting was wobbly, as if the hand that had written it was trembling. Utterson read these words:

"Dear Utterson: Four days have now passed since I received a registered letter from Henry Jekyll. That, and what followed, have aged me and weakened me so, that I must pray for enough strength to finish this letter. I swear that all I am about to relate to you happened exactly as I say.

"I was surprised to get a letter from Jekyll because I had just seen him the night before at dinner. But since he had sent it by registered post to guard against its loss, I knew it must be important. The tone of his letter was highly emotional.

"Jekyll wrote: 'Dear Lanyon, You are one of my oldest friends. It's true we have had our differences regarding scientific matters, but I would never have hesitated at any time to help you if you had appealed to me, as I am about to appeal to you. Lanyon, my life, my reason, my honor, all depend on you. If you fail me tonight, I am lost.

" 'As soon as you have read this letter, go to my house. Poole, my butler, has received written instructions and expects you. He will be waiting with a carpenter and a locksmith.

Surprised To Get a Letter from Jekyll

THE STRANGE CASE OF
DR. JEKYLL AND MR. HYDE

The door of my office is to be forced open. You will then enter alone. On the left side of the room there is a cabinet. Take out the second drawer from the top. (I am so agitated that I cannot remember if I locked the drawer or not. If it is locked, force it open.)

" 'In the drawer you will see some powders, a tube of liquid, and a notebook. I ask you to bring the drawer back to your house exactly as it is. That is the first part—and the easier of what I ask.

" 'If you start out as soon as you receive this letter, you will be back home with the drawer long before midnight. I am making allowances for unexpected delays on the way. Also, I cannot estimate too closely how long it will take to break into my office. Thus, midnight is the hour I have set for a meeting between you and the messenger I am sending. It is a good hour because your servants will be in bed. I ask that you, yourself, admit

Written Instructions

my messenger and that you receive him alone. You are to put the drawer into his hands. If these things are accomplished, you will earn my undying thanks.

" 'Five minutes afterward, if you insist on an explanation, you shall have it. You will see that these strange arrangements were absolutely necessary. If you had neglected any part, my death or my loss of reason would be on your hands.

" 'Think of me at this hour, in a strange place, fighting a distress so black that no imagination can exaggerate it. And think further that it is in your power to roll these troubles away from me as if they had never existed, simply by doing as I have asked. Serve me, my dear Lanyon, and save your friend, Henry Jekyll.

" 'P.S. I had sealed this letter when a fresh terror struck upon my soul. It is possible that the post office may fail me, and this letter

Jekyll Was Fighting a Black Distress.

not come into your hands this night. If that be the case, then do my errand tomorrow. At midnight, expect my messenger again. It may, however, be too late by then. If he does not come again, you will know that you have seen the last of Henry Jekyll.' "

Lanyon's letter continued. "I read this crazed letter several times. I felt that Jekyll had tipped over into insanity, but until that condition was proven, I would do as he requested. I went straight to Jekyll's house. There, his butler was waiting with the two workmen. He led us to Jekyll's office at the back of his laboratory.

"The carpenter shook his head when he saw the excellent wood of the door. But the locksmith had his turn first. It was fortunate that the fellow was an expert, for the lock was very difficult. It took him two hours before he could throw open the door. I entered alone, went to the cabinet, took out the drawer, and

Poole Was Expecting Lanyon.

carried it into the laboratory. The butler packed some straw over it and tied a sheet around it. Then I got into a hansom cab and brought it home.

"Here, I proceeded to examine its contents carefully. The powders were wrapped neatly enough, but not with the professional touch of a chemist. I could see that Jekyll had mixed and wrapped them himself. I opened one. It seemed to be simply a white crystalline salt.

"The glass tube was more interesting. It was half-full with a blood-red liquid that had a strong odor. I guessed that it contained phosphorus and some powerful ether, but what other things I didn't know.

"The notebook told me nothing. It was just a series of dates. Here and there the word "double" appeared, and once the words "total failure." I saw it was a record of one of Jekyll's experiments. It seemed, like so many of his other investigations and experiments, to have

Wrapping the Drawer for Safe Travel

resulted in no practical scientific usefulness.

"I asked myself how could these items in the drawer affect Jekyll's life so deeply. If his messenger could come to me, why could he not go to Jekyll's butler, as I had done? When I remembered that I was to receive this messenger in secret, I became uneasy. Even so, I sent my servants to bed. But then I loaded an old revolver so I wouldn't be completely defenseless.

"I heard my grandfather clock striking twelve at the same time that a gentle knock sounded on the front door. Opening it, I found a small man crouched against the porch pillars.

" 'Are you from Dr. Jekyll?' I asked.

"He nodded, and I told him to come in. He gave a backward glance into the night. A policeman was walking his beat not far off, and this seemed to startle my visitor. At least he entered rapidly. I closed my hand more

Lanyon Armed Himself.

tightly about the gun in my pocket and led him into the light of my office.

"He was no one I knew. He was small, and looked sickly, and I hated him on sight. Another person might have laughed because his clothes were much too large for him. He had rolled up the trouser legs to keep them off the ground. But he could make no adjustment to the jacket that sprawled across his narrow shoulders and hung to his knees.

"He was on fire with excitement. 'Have you got it? Have you got it?' he cried. He even put a hand on my arm as if to hurry an answer from me.

"At his touch, I felt an icy pang in my blood, and I stepped back. 'You forget, sir, I have not had the pleasure of your acquaintance. Please be seated,' I said.

"I sat down myself and tried to regain my usual manner of a doctor toward a patient. But it was difficult to keep down the horror

"Have You Got It? Have You Got It?"

that I had developed toward him.

"He answered with good enough manners. 'I beg your pardon, Dr. Lanyon. My impatience has robbed me of politeness. I am here at the bidding of your colleague, Dr. Henry Jekyll. I understood...' and he paused and put a hand to his throat. I could see that in spite of his calm words, he was wrestling against an approaching hysteria. '...I understood...a drawer....'

"I took pity on him and pointed to the drawer. It was behind a table and again covered by the sheet. 'There it is, sir.'

"He sprang to it, then stopped. He laid a hand on his heart. His face grew ghastly with apprehension.

"Fearing he was about to have a convulsion, I warned him gently, 'Try to compose yourself.'

"He turned a dreadful smile on me. Then, shutting his eyes and with an expression of

A Ghastly Apprehension!

despair on his face, he suddenly plucked away the sheet. When he looked in the drawer, he gave a sob of immense relief. It was a moment before he controlled himself. Then he asked in a fairly normal voice, 'Do you have a glass marked in ounces?'

"I got him the glass. Thanking me, he poured some of the red liquid into it and added a powder. The mixture began to smoke as soon as the powder melted. From red it went to deep purple. The smoking stopped, then the mixture bubbled and changed to a watery green. He nodded in approval and set the glass down on the table.

"Turning to me, he said, 'Now it's time for your decision. Shall I take this glass and leave? If I do, you will know no more than before, but you will still have the everlasting gratitude of Dr. Jekyll to make up for your unsatisfied curiosity. Or, if you wish me to stay and do what I have to, a startling new

Mixing the Powders and Liquid

area of scientific knowledge will be opened to you. Fame and power will be at your hand here in this room tonight. What you will see will stagger you. It's up to you to decide which it shall be.'

"I tried to keep my voice from shaking. 'I have come too far not to go further,' I replied.

" 'Very well,' he said. 'But, Lanyon, you must remember your medical oath. You are under the seal of secrecy.' He picked up the glass. 'And now, you who have held such narrow medical views, you who have denied the value of another doctor's research, you who have laughed at your superiors—behold!'

"He put the glass to his lips and drank it in one gulp. He cried out, staggering against the table. He clutched the back of a chair and held on, gasping, his eyes popping. He seemed to swell. His features appeared to melt and blur.

"I was standing aghast, back against the wall, away from this horror. But then I screamed

"He Drank It in One Gulp."

aloud. There, before my eyes, pale and shaken
and groping before him with his hands, like a
man tossed up on shore by a hellish
ocean—there stood Henry Jekyll!

"What he told me in the next hour, I will
not, nay, cannot, write. It sickened my soul.
My life as a man of science, as a healer of the
sick, was shaken to its roots.

"In the night I cannot sleep, and in the day
I sit terror-stricken. Death is close for me, I
know. Yet I can still hardly believe the shock
which has sent me to my end.

"I will tell you one thing, Utterson. The
creature who crept into my house that night
was, by Jekyll's own confession, known by
the name of Hyde. And he is hunted throughout England as the murderer of Sir Danvers
Carew. (Signed) Hastie Lanyon."

"There Stood Henry Jekyll!"

Utterson Now Knows the Truth.

CHAPTER 17

The Twins of Good and Evil

By the time he had finished reading Dr. Lanyon's letter, Mr. Utterson was considerably shaken. He knew now that Henry Jekyll was not in hiding as a result of killing that horrible figure stretched out in death on his office floor. The world would know only that the infamous Mr. Hyde was dead and that Dr. Jekyll had disappeared under unknown circumstances. Neither man would ever be seen again in London, though they would never leave Mr. Utterson's thoughts.

But Utterson realized that he had to know

how this tragedy had come about. Like Lanyon, he had come too far to turn back. Therefore, though his hand shook, he opened the sealed packet left to him by Jekyll and began to read the doctor's words:

"I, Henry Jekyll, was born to a large fortune and came of a good family. I was intelligent and naturally industrious. If I had a serious fault, it was a certain careless gaiety. But I surpressed this attitude as much as I could because I wanted the respect and approval of all men. Thus, in my early years I began to lead a kind of double life.

"My youthful activities were not especially sinful. In fact, another man might have boasted of such high spirits and occasional dips into a villainous life. But I had such high views that I was ashamed at the smallest fault in myself. I hid these faults, unable to admit them to public light. It caused me unrest and unhappiness. As a result, I gave much thought

The High Spirits of Youth

to the character of mankind in general.

"I did not consider myself a hypocrite—I did not try to be something I wasn't. When I tried day after day to do good and to relieve the suffering of my patients, I was myself. And when I let myself go and plunged into shameful activities, I was also myself. My scientific studies forced me to the following truth—a man is not truly one person, but actually two. But my discovery has come only part of the way. I believe that scientists who come after me will discover that a man is not only two men, but many men.

"Even before I began my experiments to prove this "two-ness" of men, I daydreamed about it. I longed to separate these two identities and place each one in its own body. Then there would be no unhappiness such as I had experienced. The upright twin could walk with his head held high, doing good, and no longer exposed to the disgrace brought about

"Every Man Is Two Men."

by his evil twin. The latter—this evil twin—could walk his downward path, free of the ideals and regrets of his good self. The struggle within a man could then cease. He would be free to be both selves.

"When I began to experiment in my laboratory, I found that certain compounds had the effect of changing a man's flesh, of waving it aside like a wind blowing curtains. I will not write down my formula for two reasons: The first reason is that my experiments were incomplete, as this document will show. I managed to reach only a certain point in dividing the twins. My second reason is that I now realize that we cannot throw off the burden of our life. We cannot experience happiness, forever untouched by troubles. When we try, even more unhappiness returns to haunt us.

"I debated a long time with myself as to whether or not to put my laboratory experi-

Jekyll Began His Experiments.

ments to a human test. I knew well that I risked death from an overdose. Finally, since the liquid was perfected, I couldn't resist. The temptation of such a discovery erased all fears of risk. I purchased the last ingredient—a large quantity of a white salt.

"Late one night, I mixed these ingredients. They smoked and bubbled and changed color. As I held that first glass in my hand, I hesitated, for I knew it might mean death to drink it. But then I quickly gulped the dose.

"Terrible pains tore through my body. I felt sick, then strange. These sensations lasted only a moment, and I then came back to myself as if from a long sickness... but with a difference! I felt younger, happier, even lighter. A new, sweet sensation came over me. I felt free to be wicked! I could be reckless and let forbidden desires take charge of me. The feeling was like wine, and I threw open my arms in welcome.

The Final Test — on a Human Being!

"I Felt Younger, Happier . . .

. . . Free To Be Wicked."

THE STRANGE CASE OF
DR. JEKYLL AND MR. HYDE

"The act of stretching my arms made me realize that the sleeves of my jacket were covering my hands. I had grown smaller! At that time, I had no mirror in my office, though I later had one installed. So I tiptoed through my own house like a burglar, intent on not waking my servants. Safe in my own room, I looked in the mirror and saw Edward Hyde for the first time.

"Let me give you my theory as a scientist as to why Hyde should be smaller and younger than Jekyll. His body had less exercise and experienced less wear, because for nine-tenths of the twins' life, Jekyll had worked hard and his body had suffered. He was now a tired, elderly man, whereas Hyde was a young man, ready to begin his life of evil.

"As I stared in the mirror, I recognized that evil written on Hyde's face. But he did not disgust me. I welcomed him. This, too, was myself. Hyde was natural and human.

Recognizing Evil on Hyde's Face

What is more—he was not a divided person. He was a single self.

"I know that anyone meeting Hyde immediately felt distaste for him. There is a reason for this. All human beings are both good and evil, but Hyde, alone, was pure evil, and people sensed this.

"I dared stay only a short time at the mirror. Hurrying back to my office, I prepared the solution again and drank it. Henry Jekyll returned.... That was the beginning.

"Perhaps if I had approached my experiments in a more noble spirit, things would have gone differently. Of the two selves within me, Jekyll was still a combination of good and evil, while Hyde was all evil. Thus, when Hyde was released, the movement of my nature could only be toward the worse side. Everything went downhill.

"From then on, I switched back and forth between my twins. When I grew bored with

"Henry Jekyll Returned."

medicine and science and my proper friends, I could instantly have the gaieties and freedom of youth as Hyde. I fell into a kind of slavery, but I loved it.

"I rented rooms in Soho. I described Hyde to Jekyll's servants, and said that he was to be obeyed and permitted the free use of the house in my absence. I even made Hyde financially secure by making him my heir in a will that shocked poor Utterson.

"So I became happy, for I could act evilly without paying the consequences. Whatever crime Hyde committed, he could be safe a moment later as Henry Jekyll, a man above suspicion. Thus, depraved, drunken, and beastly in every way, I ran wild over London as Edward Hyde. Jekyll soon found a way to soothe his conscience about all this evil, for Hyde alone was guilty, not Jekyll.

"Of course, Hyde was not always completely free from the consequences of his actions. This

"I Ran Wild over London as Edward Hyde."

was so on the night when he knocked down a child. He was so threatened by her family and some passersby that he feared for his safety. Finally, he bought them off with a check, but he had to use Jekyll's signature. The next day, I opened a checking account for Hyde by slanting my handwriting backward. Thus, he would always have money whenever he needed it.

"Some two months before the murder of Sir Danvers Carew, I had come in from a night on the town. Usually, I returned to Soho and went to sleep as Hyde. But Jekyll had an early morning appointment. So I changed back to Jekyll and slept at the doctor's house.

"In the morning I woke very early, wondering for a moment where I was. In my drowsy state I had expected to see the furnishings of Hyde's Soho rooms. When I roused myself and stretched, I caught sight of my hand. It was lean, knuckly, and covered

"I Caught Sight of My Hand."

with dark hair. But Jekyll's hand was large and well-formed and white. Terror crashed through my mind! I leapt out of bed and ran to the mirror. It was true!

"I had gone to bed as Henry Jekyll and, without tasting a drop of the mixture, I had awakened as Edward Hyde. I asked myself how this could have happened. But I had no time to speculate on scientific reasons. The important matter was to become Jekyll again. But, by now, all my servants were up, and the drugs I needed were in my office on the other side of the house. I could cover my face, but I could not conceal my shortened stature. Then I realized that if I did meet any servant, he would only be surprised at seeing Hyde in a part of the house he did not usually go into. So, I dressed quickly. A thin smile was on my lips, for as Hyde, I was bolder than Jekyll had ever been!"

Bolder Than Jekyll Had Ever Been!

Sitting Down to Breakfast as Henry Jekyll

CHAPTER 18

The Man Who Died Twice

Utterson was aghast! He put down the letter for a moment to try to make sense out of Henry Jekyll's words. But the lure of the paper in his hand was too strong to fight, so Utterson began to read again.

"Staring into Jekyll's mirror and seeing Hyde marked the beginning of the end. I ran from the bedroom to the office. I drank the mixture, and within ten minutes I was able to emerge as Henry Jekyll and sit down to his breakfast. I then realized that Edward Hyde had become stronger. And I feared that the balance between my twins might tip in favor of the evil one—permanently!

"The drug had not always acted perfectly. At first, I sometimes had to take a double dose to become Hyde. Once, it failed completely. Now the difficulty lay in holding onto Jekyll. I realized I would have to choose between the twins. The permanent Hyde would be despised and friendless, but the permanent Jekyll would give up all his evil pleasures and suffer without them. Finally, I chose the doctor, and for two months I was a kind and good man.

"Then it happened! Hyde had been caged so long that he roared out like a tiger. It was the night he lashed out at Sir Danvers. As I struck, I felt a surge of delight and could not stop until my cane broke. Then I suddenly realized that I had put my own life in jeapordy. I ran to my rooms in Soho, burned my papers, and fled. But all during the time, I delighted in my crime. I let myself into

"I Burned My Papers."

Jekyll's office and drank the drug with a song on my lips.

"I had scarcely put down the glass when Jekyll fell to his knees, filled with remorse and praying loudly. I cried and denounced my horrible twin. Now that he was a fugitive, he could never appear again at the back door. I locked it and broke the key under my heel.

"I admit that Jekyll longed for Hyde, but I kept him enclosed in me. It was too frightening to think that he was being sought all over London. But this longing finally overpowered me one day as I sunned myself on a bench in the park. A shudder shook my body, and for a moment I felt faint. This passed, but I was conscious of a sense of boldness. When I looked down, I saw my clothes loose around me and the hairy hand of Hyde clutching my hat that was too large for him.

"My reason wavered. Then Hyde, always shrewd and ready to dare, took command

"I Broke the Key Under My Heel."

where Jekyll might have given up. I had to reach my drugs, but I had locked the back door and destroyed the key. If I used the front door, my own servants would recognize Hyde and turn me over to the police. I needed help and decided on Lanyon.

"Though I was hunted, I boldly took a cab to a small hotel. There, I rented rooms and wrote letters, using Jekyll's handwriting. One letter went to Poole, the other to Lanyon. I sent them by registered mail.

"Near midnight I set out, huddled in a cab until we neared Lanyon's house. I walked the rest of the way very fast and found that Lanyon had not failed me—he had the drugs I needed. But his horror of me and what I had done added to my growing guilt.

"Then, changed back into Jekyll and once again safe in my own house, I gave thanks.

"But as I was crossing the courtyard after breakfast, the same shudder I had felt in the

Letters to Poole and Lanyon

park came over me again. I was seized by the sensations that announced the change. There was just enough time for me to rush to my office... and then Hyde stood there where Jekyll had been. It took a double dose of the drug to bring Jekyll back.

"But six hours later, I felt the pangs of change again. From that day on, I could remain Jekyll only under the direct stimulation of the drug. If I slept at night or dozed in my chair during the day, Hyde came out. I was filled with terror and hatred of him. Finally, I despaired. We were locked in mortal battle, though Hyde still found time for tricks. He scrawled horrible blasphemies in a book I admired, and he destroyed the portrait of my father.

"During the few hours that I am still able to be Jekyll, I am writing this confession. I have no hope of survival, for my supply of the drug is low. I have sent Poole all over London,

"He Destroyed the Portrait of My Father."

trying to buy the duplicate of the original salt. None has worked. I think now that the batch I first purchased had some impurity in it and that is what made the mixture work. Thus, soon Hyde will command my life completely.

"I have just used the last portion of the original salt. I will finish this confession and sit for a few last minutes as Dr. Jekyll. Then I will die, and Mr. Hyde will take over, never to be thrown off again by Dr. Jekyll. Whether Hyde will eventually be caught and die at the hands of the authorities, or whether he will have the courage to die by his own hand before that happens, I do not know. Nor do I care. It concerns a person other than myself.

"I begin to feel a faint tremor in my body. This the true hour of the death of Henry Jekyll...good-bye...good...."

"Good-bye . . . Good . . . ."